The Dark Side of Desire

Michael A. Young

ROYAL MEDIA
PUBLISHING

Royal Media and Publishing
Jeffersonville, IN 47131
http://royalmediaandpublishing.com
royalmediapublishing@gmail.com

Cover Design: Elite Covers

ISBN-13: 978-1-955501-19-4

Printed in the United States of America

Dedication

To everybody that has ever enjoyed a book.

Table of Contents

Introduction

A warm breeze rolled through the air as the sun began to set. Cars were pulling into garages; kids were being called inside for dinner and the street lights hummed as they illuminated a dim white light on the streets. Another evening has come to this common cookie cutter neighborhood. Brick houses, two car garages, small, green, well-maintained front yards, complete with ten-foot trees and picture-perfect bushes. Every yard came standard with white fences surrounding the backyards for privacy, but if you lived in one of the few houses that had a second floor, at least one of your rooms on either side overlooked someone's yard.

Just as the sky got darker and the streetlights got brighter, a lone woman came jogging down the sidewalk. In this area, seeing a woman out alone this late wasn't anything out of the ordinary. Quite a few would do so, but only one could be seen jogging home this late every evening of the week. Over the past few weeks, several bodies had been found around the city. True, the killer named the Violator had been stopped and killed, along with a serial killer who had been going from state to state, killing. He, too, was caught and killed by the police. Now, things seemed to be calming down. No city was completely murder free, but the mass amount of deaths that had plagued the city hopefully would diminish.

That one lone jogger was Alisha Kriss, a former personal trainer to the celebrities. When a star needed to get in shape for a movie, Alisha usually got the call. She wasn't cheap, but if they would stick with her routine, the results were astonishing. One of her clients, T'ondra Dove, was so jacked about her new body, she recommended Kriss to a fellow actress, Janet Smallwire. While working out, Smallwire got aggregated with Kriss and a certain tone she used, so she… accidentally… bumped a loaded barbell and it feel on Kriss' leg, causing knee damage and a leg broken in several places. Alisha was never the same after the… accident. Feeling like she wouldn't be able to truly trust a client if her tone needed to be harsh to push them, she settled on working in the gym, showing new members around and helping with meal plans.

Once in her home, Alisha laid out her nightwear and clothes for the next day. As the shower heated up, she sipped on a glass of wine and looked at her neighborhood in the bright moonlight from her bedroom window. On nights like this, she never turned-on lights upstairs because the moon was so bright. No tall trees blocked the natural light, giving her freedom to enjoy the view. When she moved in years before, she would never have her blinds open because Alisha valued her privacy. Recently, new neighbors moved in next door and they were quite interesting.

Looking out her window, she could see right into the new neighbors' back yard, right over their fence. The house on the opposite side didn't have that view; that upper window was a small port window for the bathroom. Seeing nothing was going on next door, Alisha showered, ate, then watched the news, seeing that another murder had just occurred that evening. She finished her glass of wine and went to bed.

Chapter 1

Exhibitionist

Once again, Alisha came jogging home as the streetlights brightened the sidewalks. Her pace was faster tonight and her steps hit the pavement a little harder. The day had not been a pleasant one at work, dealing with multiple difficult people, but at least she was off tomorrow. As she neared her home, she saw her neighbors were home. Following her normal routine, Alisha prepared for her shower. This time, she did her laundry first and a few other things before getting ready to shower. It was Friday night and she needed a stress relief after this day, so no wine; bourbon was the drink tonight.

Steam from the shower filled the bathroom and began to consume the bedroom. Although she loved a hot shower, Alisha needed to open the bedroom window to release some of the heat because the bourbon and heat mix was intensifying her buzz a bit too much. There was a small balcony connected to the bedroom, too, but she never used it; in fact, she hadn't opened that door since the day she moved in, when the realtor opened it while showing her around.

With the window open now, she took in the fresh night air. Then her eyes caught movement in the yard next door. The neighbors were outside, playing around. It looked like they were wearing robes. *So what, it's their yard*, she thought. Then the couple started kissing and touching. She'd never really seen what they looked like because the only time she saw them was at night doing just this—making out in the yard. Even on her off days, when she stayed home and their vehicle was there, no one was to be seen.

Alisha sipped some more of her drink while watching the couple, trying to get a glimpse of what they looked like, when she saw the woman sit down on a small stool around the patio set. The guy walked up in front of her and she parted his robe and put her head inside.

"Is she sucking his dick?" she asked herself.

The woman's head moved faster and faster, back and forth and side to side. The guy held his robe open and leaned his head back, enjoying his woman pleasing him. Wiping her lips, the woman sat up, then said something to him. With the shower still running, Alisha couldn't really hear what she said, but it kind of sounded like "it's my turn". The woman opened her legs as the man got on his knees and buried his face between her thighs.

"No doubt what he is doing to her," Alisha said as she swallowed the last gulp of liquor.

The woman untied her robe, exposing her stomach and breasts to the night air. He must have been more talented in oral sex than she was, because her moans could be clearly heard as she caressed one breast and nipple with one hand and held the back of his head with the other. Having enough foreplay, the man stood and stroked himself in front of her, or that's what it looked like from up there. The woman got up and kissed him and the two went inside.

Now sweating, Alisha took off her clothes and got into the hot shower, letting the water run all over her well-shaped body. With the oral sex display she'd just seen fresh in her mind and the liquor still in her system, her hands used the soap on her body in a different way tonight. Extra time and lather were used on her titties and nipples. Once the soap was gone, her fingers lingered around her kitten for a while. First, on top and around, then inside her honey pot. With a hand on the wall, she played and teased her clit then slid a finger inside again. In and out, then back to the clit. It didn't take long, but she gave herself a breathtaking orgasm.

Now fully relaxed, she got into bed without even putting her nightclothes on. With a smile, she thought she was going to like her new neighbors.

Chapter 2

Meeting The Tafts

A couple of days has passed and Alisha Kriss was having an excellent day at work. No one was complaining about their meal plans, and the people she had to show around the gym were very attractive men who looked like they knew their way around a gym very well. One of the cutest ones even flirted with her a tad. Usually, she would completely ignore men who did this, but it had been such a good day, she played along.

On the way home, Alisha drove with the windows down and sunroof open, with the radio playing some old school R&B. It was a nice, warm evening and the sun was about to go down soon, so she thought about riding her bicycle today instead of jogging. Driving through her neighborhood, she noticed that her new neighbors were home. As she was slowing to pull into her driveway, a car came up behind her and stopped next door.

Getting out of her car, she looked over the roof to peek at the person in the car. A young couple got out, and the man looked at his cellphone then checked the address pole in the front yard. He motioned for his lady friend to come around to his side. Seeing Alisha standing by her car, they waved to her and smiled. She politely smiled and waved back. Taking the mail out of her box, she saw that a couple of pieces were not hers. They were meant to go next door, addressed to Mr. and Mrs. Taft. Turning to see if the couple was still outside, Alisha had hoped to give them the mail to take in. Seeing the Tafts pleasuring each other in the backyard the other night, could make meeting them kind of odd.

"Well, shit! This may be something important, so I guess I'll get to meet the dynamic freak duo after all," she said to herself.

Walking down her driveway and up theirs, she stepped up onto the porch and rang the doorbell. A tall man answered the door and smiled.

"Well, hello there. Can I help you? You're our neighbor who comes by in the evenings, jogging, right?"

Taking in the guy's physique, she noticed that he was well built. Not bodybuilder big, but he could definitely move some weights. "Yes, that's me. I'm Alisha Kriss, and our mail person mistakenly put some of your mail in my box."

"Oh, really? Thank you so much for bringing it over to us. In our last neighborhood, they would've just thrown it away because it wasn't theirs."

"That's terrible. Well, no one around here would do that, or as far as I know, they wouldn't," Alisha said as she laughed and began to back down the steps.

"My name is Landon and this is my wife Marissa, and as you obviously know by the mail, we are the Tafts," he said as his wife walked up beside him.

Taking another step backwards, she answered him with a yes and said that it was a pleasure to meet them, but she didn't want to keep them. The couple said it was no bother and they were glad to meet at least one of their neighbors. Everyone seemed so nice, but most people seemed to be nice way too often. Alisha agreed and took another step down, reaching the sidewalk.

Marissa told Alisha that she didn't have to run off and she was welcome to come in for a drink, or at least water, after her jog. Alisha politely told her thank you, but that she needed to get in, to shower. *Also,* she thought to herself, *I'm sure the sweat from my exit parts wouldn't be a pleasant smell.*

"Well, Mrs.—"

"No, it's Ms."

"Well, Ms. Kriss, stop by anytime. We'll usually here, inside or out, getting into something fun."

Alisha thought of what type of fun they have outside and smiled as she waved bye then walked to her own house. Going up her steps, she glanced over her shoulder to see if the Tafts were still in the doorway, looking. Fortunately, they had gone back to their own business and closed the door.

After a hot shower and healthy meal, Alisha watched the news before going to bed. The top story tonight was another body found. She rubbed her eyes and shook her head, then turned off the television and went to sleep.

Chapter 3

Super Freaks

Another week was ending and Alisha was just finishing another jog. Coming up her street, she glanced over at the Tafts' and noticed another car in the driveway. Slowing, trying to brush a stain off her leggings, she thought to herself, *that's odd. For as long as they have been living here, albeit not that long, the Tafts have company over again. I wonder if they are super freaks like the Tafts.* Happy she wasn't seen, but curious at the same time, she went up her steps, checked the mail and went inside.

Being a creature of habit, Alisha showered, ate and watched TV in bed. As she was drifting off to sleep, the sound of people talking and laughing broke her sleepiness. Thinking of what she had seen the last time the Tafts were outside late, she got up to peek out the window. Since her room was dark and no lights were on in their backyard, she knew no one would see her. They still had company. This late?

The Tafts were playing around again, then embraced to give each other a passionate kiss. The other couple did the same. Then, to Alisha's surprise, the other lady came over and kissed Landon then kissed Marissa. The guy followed and kissed Marissa too. Landon took the woman aside and sat her on a patio table. He pulled her pants off and she opened her legs, lying back. Landon placed his face right between her thighs.

What the hell? Alisha thought, but her attention was now drawn to Marissa on her knees, in front of the other guy, performing oral sex. From Alisha's vantage point, that's what it looked like, anyway. Who was she kidding? Marissa had another man's penis in her mouth while her husband had his tongue in another woman's crotch.

"My new neighbors are pure freaks, and now they are having freak parties!"

Wanting to ignore what she was seeing but unable to move away, Alisha found herself oddly being turned on. With a mind of its own, her hand began to caress her breasts. One hand pinched a nipple while the other slid through short, silky hair between her legs, through her panties. Hidden in the shadows of her bedroom window, Alisha was free to do as she pleased to herself.

Landon now had the woman bent over in a lawn chair, giving her slow thrust from behind. The guy Marissa was giving head to now was holding her up in the air. Her back was to her husband, with no concern to his activities, just to her own pleasure. Her moans were soft but loud enough for any ears that were listening to hear, like Alisha's. The window had been slightly opened for the purpose of trying to hear any sounds of passion. It was getting late and the other neighbors were older so, at this time of night, they would be asleep.

Landon was looking over the other woman's body, when he raised his head to catch a night breeze, to dry the sweat on his face, and noticed Alisha in the window. He didn't focus on her because he didn't want to scare her away. Knowing he had an audience, now made this even more exciting. His penis got a little harder and a little thicker. He glanced up and over a couple seconds too long, and they locked eyes.

At first, Alisha hid herself, but she looked out again after a minute or two. He was still looking up at her window, giving himself to the woman from the back. The woman never opened her eyes.

"He must have some good dick," Alisha said to herself.

Noticing that she was watching again, Landon started going faster and faster as well as harder. Holding the woman's waist, pulling her back as he pushed forward, her large breasts swung back and forth. Alisha could barely make out what she was saying, but it sounded like, "I'm coming." She gripped the top of the chair and let out a "fuck!" that was clearly heard. Landon then pulled himself out and took off a condom, or that's what it looked like from the window, and ran over to his wife who was on her knees again. After exploding all over Marissa's face, he massaged her breasts from behind as the other guy did the same and came all over her breasts. Smiles and giggles came from all four as they went back inside, satisfied.

Horny and wet now, Alisha closed the drapes to the window and used a toy in bed until she, too, was satisfied and went to sleep.

Chapter 4

That's Strange

After another long and physical jog, Alisha made her way back through the neighborhood. Coming up on the Tafts' house, she noticed their guests' vehicle was still there. *Must be going for another round tonight,* she thought. Unintentionally slowing, her mind played out a possible sex scene that could go down later. Then Marissa came out the door, heading to the guests' vehicle.

"Oh, hi there, Alisha. Those jogs you go on are really keeping you in wonderful shape."

"Thank you, Marissa. If I don't keep myself in shape, no one else will do it for me."

"You are absolutely amazing, and if you don't mind me saying, your ass and breasts look scrumptious."

Taken aback by the compliment, Alisha lost her next words and just stared at Marissa, thinking, *is she flirting with me?* Mrs. Taft was a freak, that she knew for sure, but she had no proof that she was into women. When she walked away, she noticed Marissa getting into the guests' vehicle. Maybe they said it was okay to use it.

Pulling off, Marissa spoke out the window. "Did you know that you lost that beautiful head scarf you left the house with?"

"Oh yeah. It got caught on a branch and tore, so I just left it on that branch."

"Well, that's a shame, dear. Hope you can find another. You looked so hot in it." Then Marissa pulled away in her company's vehicle. Alisha walked up to her steps and looked back down the street as the car disappeared around the corner. Shaking her head as if she was shaking out crazy thoughts, Alisha went inside then stopped to look out the window as if she was trying to let her mind understand what her eyes had just witnessed.

After going through her usual routine, she lay in bed to watch the news, only to hear of another murder victim being found. Alisha had become numb to the almost daily reports of bodies being found. Before she could drift off to sleep, her mind just couldn't let go of why her neighbors' company would leave their vehicle. They couldn't be family, considering what they did in the backyard. Well, for some people, that type of shit was okay and normal, but where she was from, that was just sick.

With her bedroom window being open and the dead silence of the night, the sound of a car pulling in close by was crystal clear. Maybe it was Marissa or her company coming back. Getting out of bed, she looked out a window where she could see their driveway. It was Landon… and Marissa… in his car! What the hell? Where was the other car? Calming herself, she realized Marissa was dropping off the car and Landon had picked her up.

As they got out, another car pulled in behind them. A beautiful woman stepped from her car and looked around the neighborhood in the chilly night air. The woman hugged Marissa, then kissed her and did the same to Landon. After a squeeze of both women's asses, they all went inside.

Chapter 5

Something Is Not Right!

It was the weekend and Alisha decided not to go in to work for overtime today. She was exhausted and wanted to get in an easy, early run then rest with a good book, a good movie to watch, tasty food and a bottle of wine. Just as she got dressed to go out, she saw Landon drag a large black bag around the side of the house to the front and toss it in the trunk of the woman's car.

Alisha said out loud, "Now, what the hell is this? Why is he putting garbage in that lady's trunk? Where is that woman?"

A thought came across her mind. *Maybe that was… the woman! Nah, couldn't be. They didn't fuck the woman to death and are now trying to get rid of the body, are they?*

Forgetting she was in the front window now, in broad daylight, and could be seen very easily, Alisha gazed on like a nosey old woman watching bad kids.

Landon turned and saw he was being watched and froze for a second. A second only, then he waved to Alisha. She was surprised he noticed her, then it hit her that she was looking out a big window and could easily be seen, so she gave a small wave back and left the window.

That night as she prepared for bed and undressed to shower, she heard the news say a body was found in a black bag, down by the dumpsters outside the sports arena. Hearing this, made Alisha pause and then run and sit down in front of the TV. Looking over towards the window that overlooked the neighbors' back yard, she got up to take a look.

There, outside again, were the Tafts, with a woman sitting on the table. Alisha went over to turn the TV off so she could be nosey in the darkness. She couldn't tell if it was the same woman or not, but what she could tell was

Landon and Marissa had their heads between the woman's legs and her head was back. Evidently, she was enjoying whatever they were doing to her. Landon rose first, then his wife. The woman and Marissa held hands and kissed, then went inside. Landon mouthed something to them and sat down to finish a drink he had. With legs wide open, he held his half-hard man muscle as he finished the drink. He caught a glimpse of someone looking down on him from next door. He knew who it was but made no effort in trying to cover himself. Instead, he kept looking at the window and began to stroke himself slowly.

As Alisha watched, a small tingle began to grow between her thighs. She could plainly see he was getting harder, and from that vantage point, to see it grow must mean Landon's penis was absolutely huge. The tingle now turned into a throb and it was increasing more and more. Against her will, she let her hand go through the wet playground under her waist.

Just as Alisha teased herself, the moonlight broke from the clouds and gave light to her show. Landon watched and rubbed faster. Not paying attention to what he was looking at, the female company came back out. Seeing his manhood very stiff in his hand, she bent over and immediately swallowed his erection.

Still with his eyes on Alisha, Landon exploded in the mouth of the woman who was tasting him. Alisha circled her swollen magic button with her wet finger, hoping to see Landon use his large tool one more time, but the woman stood up, blocking her view. What she couldn't see, was the woman looking Landon in the eyes as she licked her lips and swallowed every single drop of the human cream in her mouth. By this time, Marissa came back to the doorway and motioned for the two to come inside. She was wearing a thin robe, but it was hanging open and she was nude under it. Her husband came past first and gave a quick suck to one of her nipples, then went in. The woman was next. Marissa gave her a passionate kiss with tongue, then they both went inside and closed the door.

Alisha was now far too horny to just go to sleep. Now that the Taft show has moved inside, she needed a way to release. Moving from the window, she lay on the bed and pulled a toy that had pulsation, vibration, and rotation from the nightstand. With a mental image of Landon's penis, she sent herself off to the land of ecstasy before falling asleep.

Chapter 6
What Are They Into?

The next morning, Alisha sat at work with her mind far from the task she was supposed to be doing. Sitting at a long table in an office alongside several men in basic color suits, never being basic, Alisha sat in a chair near the head of the table, representing class and style, in an electric blue suit with a striped bone white and candy apple red top. Also, candy apple red, five-inch heels. As stunning as she looked, her attention was not on the boring meeting, but on the sex act she had watched and partly participated in the night before.

"Ms. Kriss, what is your opinion on how to handle this situation? "

"Situation? What situation, Mr. Musa?"

"Ms. Kriss, the situation of the company possibly being a victim of a hostile takeover and all of us losing our jobs? Well, most of us."

"Oh, that? Sorry, my mind was elsewhere. All these bodies being found are very troubling. I suggest that we not worry about it too much. We are one of many companies being eyed for takeover. Our clientele, which is impressive, is not quite the moneymaker they really are looking for. They seem to want a company with huge moneymaking potential, but not on a strong foundation. Though we are doing well, the Wisbell company is looking for a much more profitable and easier obtainable company. Why go after the million dollar company when you can take over a multimillion dollar company, like Inner Global Tech?"

"That makes sense, Ms. Kriss. Let's hope you are correct."

The meeting went on for another half hour and Alisha couldn't wait to get out. Normally, she looked forward to her evening routines, but now, she had a curious hunger for more of her neighbors' sexual antics. Who knows, maybe she'd masturbate with a light behind her this time. Who was she kidding? What were the chances of them doing something like that again tonight?

Alisha's jog just didn't have the same excitement today. She actually ran a bit faster than usual so that she could get home and prepare. Coming up the street, she looked over at the Tafts' driveway and saw no vehicles. Disappointed, she stopped running by their mailbox. Alisha jumped when a car horn sounded behind her. The Tafts blew and waved as they pulled in. When they got out, she saw a different woman getting out from the backseat.

She thought to herself, *this evening has just gotten a whole lot better and interesting.* Alisha waved back and began to jog again as she went home. Once inside, she glanced out the window to get a good look at the fresh meat being brought in to the Tafts' den of sex. The woman strolled in the house, walking between Landon and Marissa. Marissa was holding her hand while Landon patted and rubbed her luscious rear end.

"Where the hell do they find these women? Are they using some kind of app or freaky people meet site?" After watching the trio touch and fondle each other as they went inside, she decided to go ahead and do her normal routine. During her shower time, Alisha was tempted to get to work and release some sexual electricity, but knowing the habits of her neighbors, why waste it in the shower when she could get off to a live show.

The clock ticked and nothing was happening next door. Well, nothing she could see, anyway. Alisha had gotten herself well-prepared for another peep show. Wearing a purple lace bra and thong panty set, she sipped a glass of red wine. She wanted to get a buzz, to loosen up a bit. Her body was on point and she knew it; with all the running she did, her thighs were thick and strong. Just when the temptation of her favorite toy was almost too great to resist, the doorbell rang.

Looking at a clock on the dresser, she saw that it was 10:37pm. Alisha grabbed a robe on the way down to the door. When she opened it, to her surprise, Marissa was standing there.

Shocked, she took a step back. "Mrs. Taft... is everything okay?"

"Sorry to bother you so late. I hope I didn't wake you and, yes, everything is fine. Sort of, and call me Marissa, honey."

"What can I help you with?"

"Lan and I, mostly Lan, needs your assistance really quick. If you have time?"

"I wasn't in bed yet. I'll try to help y'all if I can."

"We would appreciate it so much, and I promise it will be only a hot second."

Alisha closed her door and followed Marissa to her home. She opened the door and the two went inside. Following Marissa through a hallway, they entered a room with a soft blue light. Landon was on the bed, buried up to his ears in the other woman's pussy. It felt like a vacuum had just removed the breath from her lungs and her eyes were frozen open.

She tried to speak..."I-I… what, wha— Why am I? Am I supposed to?"

Marissa laid her hand on Alisha's shoulder to calm her. "No, dear. You're not here to join in, just spectate. Landon here was feeling extra adventurous and wanted someone to watch." Marissa strolled through the blue lit room over to the bed and stopped. "He said he saw you in the window one night when we were out." Making sure not to alert the new woman of their previous sexual encounters, she never mentioned the other women, just the fact that Landon had seen her while outside. "So, who better than you, to bring closer to the action?"

Marissa then lay across the bed, rolled Landon to the side, and tasted his hard penis like an overheated person enjoying an ice-cream cone. The other woman reached down and began to caress the slippery slit between Marissa's legs. After a few moments of body dining by everyone, they took new positions. Landon was slowly pushing himself into the woman while his wife was flicking a nipple with quick, wet tongue strokes and gently pinching the other.

Alisha sat in a chair across from the bed. Her breath returned but was very heavy and excited. The live action porno being performed before her eyes caused her body to act on its own. Her robe fell open and lay on the side of her curvaceous breasts. Her nipples were hard and about to come through her silk bra like caramel knives. A very toned leg hung over each arm of the chair as her hands trailed her inner thighs, going up and down. A finger slid under the thong panties, slowly sinking into her shallow wishing well. With one finger in, the thumb teased that button which would launch ecstasy throughout her pelvic region.

As he took pleasure in satisfying this stranger they'd invited into their bed, Landon watched as his wife licked, sucked and nibbled on her breasts. Removing himself slowly from her hungry, juicy peach, he moved behind his wife and pushed her back down, then aggressively inserted his man muscle in her neglected opening. The woman rotated to where she could indulge herself with Marissa's breasts while hers were enjoyed at the same time.

Pumping, Landon locked eyes with Alisha. He felt himself extend at least an inch and swell slightly also. Marissa moaned with this new burst of flesh inside her. His thrusts were so furious that it caused his wife to crawl on top of the woman until lips were over sticky lips. Her tongue danced and darted in the woman while she held the part of Landon that was swinging and thumping against the back of Marissa's ass.

Alisha matched his movements with her finger as if he was inside her. A small pool had begun to collect in the chair between her legs which brought an early explosion from Landon. He exited his wife and threw off the condom. The two women lay exhausted side by side as he showered them with thick ounces of lust rain. Then they all looked over at Alisha. She was about to let her little kitty scream when her mind took back her body. Embarrassed, she looked everyone in their faces then got up and sprinted out the house and home.

Slamming her door and dashing to the bed, her mind revisited every emotion she'd just experienced. Ashamed of herself but excited at the same time, she thought, *what the hell was I just a part of?* Sleep finally found her, but it took a long time to do so.

Chapter 7
No! They Can't Be

The next morning while getting ready for another boring day at work, Alisha looked at her neighbors' home through the blinds in her bedroom window. Vivid images of the sexual performance she had witnessed last night still played in her mind. The temptation to join in was high but out of the question. If she had known what was going on over there, no way would she have gone. Well… Then the daydream was erased by movement in the Tafts' backyard.

Alisha took a sip of the coffee she'd been enjoying, reheating and sipping again. Landon was taking out the trash. A puzzled look came across her face as she remembered that trash day wasn't for another two days. Maybe the can inside was full, but that was a big damn bag of trash. Plus, he was dragging it. A person wouldn't drag a regular bag of trash, because it could split and scatter garbage everywhere. There was something else in there.

She said aloud, "Oh God!! That woman last night. Just like that late night I saw a big bag being brought out before!"

Did they murder that woman? Is that what they do? Is that part of their freaky desires? Then she peered closer at the backyard as she took a longer sip of the hot beverage. She faintly heard Marissa's voice coming from somewhere near the front of the house. It sounded like she was talking to someone.

The hushed voice got quieter, then the sound of a vehicle starting filled the morning air. After swallowing, Alisha spoke out again. "Okay. I guess she is taking that woman home, or at least back to her vehicle."

While at work, Alisha couldn't concentrate, because too many things were colliding in her mind. This damn project she was working on, with no real assistance, her neighbors' weird behavior and their exhibitionist lifestyle. Not to mention, how sexually arousing that experience was. Then the black bags being brought out. Until the night she watched the sex from her window, the random murders in the woods where she would jog was a concern. Now, that seemed to fade away, out of importance.

Leaving work early, Alisha went home to change and get a quick run in. As she did, a woman wearing a very thin, bright yellow body suit came walking towards her. Alisha tried to ignore the woman, but even at a distance, she could tell the woman was outside, wearing damn near body lace, alone on a trail where several women had been murdered. On top of that, the woman had nothing on underneath. The print between her legs and hard nipples could be seen from space. Alisha thought as she approached the woman, *I'd bet she would be the type of person to be down for a freaky ass threesome.*

Coming off the trail from out of the woods, Alisha brushed some leaves off her shoes then continued along until she reached the end of her street. Trying to look off into the distance, namely the Tafts' driveway, a vehicle slowed as it came up behind her. Looking over her shoulder, she balled up her fist with one hand and reached toward the pouch strapped to her waist. The vehicle stopped next to her and the window came down.

"Hey, Alisha. How you doing? Can we talk if you have a few seconds?"

"Oh hello, Marissa. Sure. I have a few."

Marissa motioned for her to come get in on the other side. She drove slowly toward their homes and finally spoke. "Are you all right after our show for you?"

Not knowing how to tell her neighbor that she was so sexually charged from it that her body was still tingling, she simply said, "I'm fine. It w-was… it was unexpected and interesting…" Then her voice trailed off.

Pulling into her driveway, Marissa put the gear into park. She leaned back in her seat and looked over at Alisha. "You know… if you enjoyed it and are feeling adventurous, you are more than welcome to join us." Then she smiled.

Alisha was blushing, remembering the pool of lust that was left in her panties after seeing the pure ecstasy in the woman's face as the Tafts had their way with her. Also, a chill shot down her spine that caused goose bumps to rise on her arm as she thought about the mysterious bags and never seeing the guests leave. Not wanting to alarm Marissa of her knowing about the bags, she managed to smile and answer. "Well. How about you let me think about it and keep the option open?"

"Fair enough. Believe me, it will be an experience to die for." Marissa then opened her door and got out, followed by Alisha.

Inside her own house, Alisha dropped her keys on the counter and went upstairs. Following her normal routine, she undressed as she walked. Picking up the TV remote before hitting the shower, she turned on the news as usual.

"The woman, who is yet unidentified, was found in the woods, just off the trail. This makes the fifth victim this month."

"Damn!" Alisha shouted as she tossed the remote onto the bed. After a quick shower, light meal and about three hours of just flipping channels, she thought about calling it a night. Curiosity caused her to get up and move back the curtain, to get a peek at the Tafts' yard. With only the light from the television on, she stood in the window, naked. Looking and searching for possible activities, her breathing became rapid and her nipples began to swell. She could feel her heartbeat between her legs as moisture formed. A few minutes passed, and nothing. Just when she was about to give up, a faint, dim light appeared from what she guessed was the Tafts' bedroom.

Alisha instantly got wet. Two beads of anticipation ran down her thigh. First, Marisa appeared in the window with her bare chest pressed against the window, but no sign of anyone else. No husband, no extra woman, just her. Then Landon's head came up in front of her. Not all the way up, but just enough to see the top of his head. It looked like she held on to something above her head, because she lifted one leg and put it on the window sill. Landon's head bobbed up and down and in circles, causing Marissa to howl in lust-filled excitement. Alisha could hear her joy all the way over at her house.

Alisha wanted to touch herself, but she also wanted to rush over and feel what she was feeling more. Then, after he was finished dining on his wife's sweet wine, they moved from the window and into the shadows of the bedroom. Disappointed, Alisha quivered from an orgasm that had built up and was now being wasted. Going back to bed, she refused to toy herself. She was going to hold on to this cherry bomb until something happened that would cause it to blow. Fading into sleep, she said, "The fuse is lit now." Then she fell asleep with a grin.

Chapter 8

Something's Wrong

Once again at work, Alisha was sitting in a meeting with her mind far away from the business at hand. Freddy Jowl stood in front of everyone, rambling on, going over the same damn chart and impossible quarter projection for an hour. It didn't make sense when he started and sure as hell didn't make any more sense an hour later. Karolin Stack was across the table eying Mitchell Cain, but he was more interested in his phone. The director of operations, Dennis O'Bannon, rocked back and forth in his seat at the head of the V-shaped business table.

"Freddy? We need to wrap up this meeting before a new year starts, could you speed it along or end it? Your choice, but make a choice now!"

"Yes, sir, Mr. O'Bannon." Freddy talked a little more then sat down.

O'Bannon ended the meeting and cautioned everyone about being careful if they were an outdoors exerciser. There had been too many bodies of runners and bikers found on the nearby trails over the last month. As they walked out of the conference room, Karolin caught up to Alisha after Mitchell completely ignored her while he still scrolled on his phone. Karolin didn't know it, but Mitchell had his eyes and mind on the nude picture site he was browsing. Basically, Karolin didn't have the right equipment below the waist that he liked.

"Ah, Alisha, what do you think is up with Mitch? He is always on that phone during every meeting, unless he is speaking."

Alisha couldn't care less and was annoyed, so she looked at her and just shrugged her shoulders and kept walking.

With a smirk, Karolin said, "He's probably mesmerized by those nude pics I've been sending him."

Now, Alisha looked over at her and raised an eyebrow. "Nudes? To Mitch?"

"Girl, don't tell anyone. I normally don't do things like that, but I really want a sample of his—"

Before she could finish, Alisha said, "You know Mitchell is gay?"

"Gay? Bullshit. He doesn't look gay or act gay. He's just playing games."

Alisha just giggled while she patted Karolin's shoulder and told her keep trying then walked into her office. Sitting down, she threw her head back and closed her eyes. Sex and fantasies of what could happen if she let herself get sucked into her neighbors' wild sexual appetite were on her mind. Her neighbors, her damn neighbors, why did she never see their guests leave? Why didn't any of them drive their own vehicles? More importantly, what the hell was in those bags? They were big, but not big enough for a body. *I don't think.*

Alisha glanced over at the clock on the desk and saw she had been daydreaming for at least an hour and it was past time to go. She decided to skip the run for today and outright ask the Tafts together about their partners and the bags.

Chapter 9

The Seduction

By the time Alisha got home, she was more determined than ever to get to the bottom of the mysterious vanishing guests and large black bags. When she pulled up, she noticed they weren't home yet. Probably out searching for a new victim. As she paced around her home, Alisha sipped a glass of wine which turned into two, then three. Eventually, the bottle was empty and she was very tipsy. Looking out the window, she was surprised to see that the Tafts' car was now in their driveway. When the hell did they pull up? She had been watching for the last twenty to thirty minutes, or so she thought. Looking at the clock on the wall, Alisha saw that she had been drinking and pacing for the last two hours. She wasn't drunk, but she was buzzing.

Slurring her words, she spoke to herself out loud. "I don't know what the fuck is going on over there, but I'm about to find out!"

Stumbling out the door, she walked over to the house next door. As she went up the walkway and reached out to ring the doorbell, she saw that the door was partially open. A sense of panic went up her spine. Maybe someone broke in. It wasn't the fear of the killer in the woods on the path, but this was *what if someone was trying to rob them…*

Pushing the door open, she saw that all the lights were out. She wanted to call out, but it might alarm anyone who might be in there who shouldn't be. Sneaking through the house, she was definitely feeling the effects of that whole bottle of wine. *Where the hell is everybody?* she thought. Peeking out the backdoor, she saw no one out there, either. Confused, she stood there and guessed they might have gone to their prey's home for a change. Then she heard a faint moan coming from somewhere underneath her feet. Alisha picked up a heavy object sitting on a table as a weapon and walked around until she found a door with a faint purple light under it.

Alisha held her weapon, ready to strike, as she slowly walked down the steps. Entering the basement room, her eyes widened and her jaw dropped. Before her, she saw the Tafts and another guy. Marissa was strapped into some kind of contraption hanging from the ceiling, with her husband behind her, holding her waist and pounding away while the other guy was standing in front of her matching Landon's motions. Alisha dropped her weapon, causing all eyes to move in her direction, but no one stopped what they were doing. She watched as Landon slowly pulled his long, hard muscle out of his wife and unbuckled the straps holding her. The guy looked at the Tafts and removed the straps holding her front as his penis began to decrease in size.

Marissa and Landon walked over to Alisha and held her hand and shoulder. Landon put her hand on his thick, sticky penis and guided it as he used it to stroke himself. Marissa took Alisha's ear in her mouth and massaged her breasts under her shirt—which was easy, because in her buzzed state, she had come over in a short, mid-cut t-shirt and tiny track shorts. Marissa kissed her passionately on the lips, followed by her husband. Now in a state of mixed emotions of surprise and excitement, she allowed them to lead her to a large, soft ottoman in a corner just past a bed.

Before they sat her down, Marissa pulled her shorts off and Landon removed her shirt. Her large chest and sublime ass caused the extra guy in the room to regain his erection. Both Tafts took a nipple in their mouths and sucked and nibbled. The guy slowly stroked himself, hoping to be invited in with the new visitor. The Tafts gently pushed her down on the ottoman and Marissa kneeled in front and opened her legs. Alisha looked down as Marissa treated her honey pot like a young bear treats a honeycomb. Landon stood next to Alisha with his more than impressive member very close to her face. She stared at it, licking her lips.

Landon held his penis in his hand as he traced her mouth with it before letting it slide past her lips. The pleasure she received from being tasted sent enough signals to her brain to ignore the fact she was now trying to use the warmth of her mouth to melt the human popsicle. The man standing alone eyed Marissa as she arched her back and spread her legs, inviting him to enter. Sliding on a fresh condom, he pushed himself inside the soft, wet opening. Marissa paused her tongue work for a second as she felt the man's muscle diving deep inside her.

"Shit! Your dick is big! Fuck it like it's yours!"

The guy's strokes became more forceful as he reached around and held Marissa's hand-sized breast. Landon removed himself from Alisha, to her displeasure, and walked behind her. With a hand against her back, he physically suggested she lean forward. She did what was implied, lying chest down. She heard plastic opening and saw it fall next to her, then her opening was parted by rubber covering the biggest thing she had ever felt.

The rush of ecstasy can cause a person to do crazy things. Alisha watched Marissa's breasts swing as her nipples danced just inches away.

"Suck them," she heard from behind as Landon kept a slow, steady rhythm.

First, with a flick of the tongue, then a tight lip lock, she took in the hard nips. Landon removed himself and so did the other guy. Immediately, Alisha wondered if the guys were now going to fuck each other while the girls watched or took care of each other, but they passed the other without a word and she saw Landon remove his condom.

"You know I have to finish in this ass." Then he saw Marissa's eyes roll up in her head as that long thing went into her butt.

Forgetting about the other guy, Alisha was taken by surprise to feel his hands on her thighs as he entered her vagina. While he glided all the way in, she tightly gripped the ottoman because the dick in her now was even bigger than Landon's.

"Oh shit, this juicy is amazing." Hearing this, her opening acted as if it had its own mind and tightened around the visitor inside her, causing him to fall backwards, snatching off the condom and exploding all over himself. Marissa embraced Alisha's ass and bit on her sweaty nipple as her husband came all over her ass and back.

Chapter 10
What Was That?

Lying in bed just watching the ceiling fan go around and around, her mind tried to erase and replay the events of just a few hours ago. Morally, it was so wrong, but it had been intensely satisfying. It never would have happened if she wasn't half drunk, or would it? Did she want to have sex with the Tafts? Landon, maybe? Secretly, she might have, after seeing that woman using his cock like a straw in the backyard. That woman... what happened to her? The other woman too? What about that big-dicked guy from tonight?

Getting up, she looked out the window and saw her neighbors carrying a big black bag out the backdoor. Then she could make out what looked like a shoe hanging out of a hole in the bag.

"Oh my God! I knew it; I damn well knew it. They are murderers."

They went back in, then reappeared, both holding another bag, even bigger. Just before they tossed it in the garbage can, it fell open. Piles and piles of clothes hit the ground. Old clothes.

"Marissa, I told you we should have donated these damn clothes years ago. Then we wouldn't have to move this shit out of the way for our play things."

"I know, I know, Lan, but wasn't it you who said these old things might come back in style?"

Landon laughed as he finished picking up the clothes from the ground. He slapped his wife on the ass as they went back inside.

Alisha let out a big sigh of relief and dropped her head. Forgetting that she'd never turned the TV off from when she was drinking earlier, she heard the late news reporting about a body being found just outside of the wooded area where she jogged. Snapping her head around, she said, "What the fuck!"

Lying in her bed and sweating like hell, Alisha rolled around and squirmed, trying to find that cool spot on the mattress. Frustrated, she sat up and saw the shadow of a person in her bedroom doorway. Squinting to focus, she saw the man walk closer. It was Landon. She tried to yell, but excitement kept the sound in her throat. He was bare naked and that long piece of meat swung between his legs as he came closer. Someone was behind him. She figured it was Marissa, but the figure stepped around, and it was another guy. He looked like a body builder and was also nude.

"Landon! What are you doing? Why are you in my bedroom? How did you get in here?"

As they came closer, another man entered. Excitement turned to fear now. They surrounded her bed as she looked at all of them. All three were naked and their dicks hung so low, they touched her bed as they stood over it.

"Please, don't rape me! Please get out of my house!"

Landon leaned over the end of the bed and told her, "We're not here to rape you. We are going to love you."

Then the two unknown men slowly pulled apart her nightgown and started sucking her breasts. Landon climbed on the bed, opened her legs and buried his face between her sweaty thighs. While enjoying the taste of her luscious, soft titties, both men took a hand of Alisha's and placed it on their iron-hard pipes. She slowly stroked each of them while Landon continued his meal of her flesh.

"I think it's wet enough now." Landon pushed himself up and forward, to let his pleasure tool dive deep inside the juicy mount. As she moaned, one of the men dropped his enormous penis into her mouth. Alisha treated the object in her mouth like a baby treats its first pacifier. Then after a short time, the other man inserted his after the other stranger. The whole time, Landon pumped away.

The experience was so thrilling, but when she rode the tallest of the men, the other climbed behind her and slowly placed his cock in her ass. Alisha's eyes rolled and her mouth opened. This gave Landon the opportunity to finally get himself sucked on. It was like a rhythmic motion to see all four in action.

"Oh God, my pussy is about to explode." She could feel a body-numbing orgasm building. Just when she was at her climax, the three men released their lust at the same time, all over her, then she released.

Alisha's body violently jerked, waking her from the erotic dream she was having. She sat up and realized there was no one in her room and there never was. She now lay in bed in a puddle of her own immense orgasm residue. Sweating, she gave one more small jerk, and her honey pot gave another squirt. Now too worn out to even shower, she snatched off the sheets and her panties. She sighed, curled up clinching the pillow, then dropped back off to sleep.

Chapter 11
Giving In To Desire

Alisha was about to leave work when she heard a group of people down the hall talking about the recent string of murders in the city. Every city had their fair share of violent deaths, but this cluster of random attacks in one area was highly unusual. From the time the trail through the wooded area was cleared and widened, runners from all over the city had used it. The murders weren't exactly gruesome, but they don't need to be. A few had sliced throats, and a couple had metal spikes to the heart.

"Did you hear about the murder last night? The young man was found under some bushes."

"Yes, I saw that on news this morning. What is this world coming to?"

Hearing *young man found dead*, Alisha's ears perked up. Her mind went right to the black bags she had seen the Tafts carrying out, but seeing the pile of clothes and hearing them speak of all the clothes, made her think it couldn't be their company from last night.

"Oh, hi there, Alisha, have you heard—"

"Yes, I did. I go through there almost every day. Late evening, matter of fact, and I've never been worried about being attacked."

Then Freddy walked up and said, "With thick thighs like those, I'll bet you wouldn't have any problem outrunning anyone after you." Then he looked her up and down, pausing at her large, firm bottom, and on up her body, to a look that Medusa would envy.

"No, Freddy, I wouldn't worry about anyone chasing me! I would turn and kick someone's balls up to their lungs. I doubt they would be much harm after that. Would you like a demonstration?"

Just the thought of the act, made Freddy's stomach instantly hurt. "No thank you, I completely believe you." Then he walked away awkwardly, as if he'd just taken that kick from Alisha.

The women looked at each other and laughed. Even Alisha had a huge grin on her face. They said their "have a good evening" and "be safe going home" then all left the office floor to go home.

The ride home was a slow one. Alisha had no plans to run today—a combination of the latest body found and her honey pot still pulsating from the large piece of manhood that was in her the night before. She had never been with a woman, either, nor had she desired to do so. Marissa had done things to her no man had ever matched. Then the softness of her breasts in her mouth and the sounds of pure ecstasy Marissa made when she touched her, enticed her to do more, but only if more was done to her. Then she shook her head as if trying to actually shake the thought from her head.

"I'm not a lesbian," she said aloud.

Driving through her neighborhood, she passed the Tafts' home. Their vehicle was there.

What the hell do they do? Where do they work? Or do they even work? They seem to be always here.

In her driveway now, Alisha shut off the car and went into the house. She went to the kitchen and opened the refrigerator to decide what she would fix for dinner that night. She sat for a second after dinner plans were made. She thought of the guy she used to date and how she had come home early and found him on the couch ramming a young nineteen-year-old girl from the neighborhood. Bad enough he was cheating in her home, no less, but the bastard had a mask on and was streaming the sex online. So, the viewers got to see the two of them get their asses beaten live, by Alisha. She told him she would kill him for that, but he didn't take her seriously until the day Alisha walked up on him with a loaded gun one night, after leaving amateur night at the strip club. She pulled the trigger, but it jammed. He was so scared that he turned to run from her and ran right into a drunk driver speeding thought the parking lot. Blood showered everyone close by, including Alisha. No one saw her pull the gun on him, so it was determined he was killed accidentally by a drunk driver. She'd smiled at the sight of his crumpled, broken and bloody body.

She was snapped out of her thoughts by the doorbell. Alisha blinked several times and looked around until she realized what she'd just heard. Getting up, she answered the door and Marissa greeted her. She stood on the porch, wearing a beautiful, long satin robe. Her hair was down and lay over her shoulders.

"Excuse me, dear, I hope I didn't interrupt you from something."

"Oh. No, no, I was just deciding what I was going to eat."

"Well, Landon and I were about to do the same. I fixed way more food than we can eat, as usual. You are welcome to come over and dine with us."

Alisha considered the invitation and thought that not cooking would be great, and just before she could answer, Marissa spoke.

"Please? We would love to have the company."

"Okay, sure…"

Marissa stepped back and opened her robe, exposing her naked body. Toned thighs and firm breasts were on full display in the fading evening light. A sudden breeze rushed by, causing the naked nipples to stiffen. "I think dessert may end up being the best part." Then she winked and turned to leave.

The secret treasure between Alisha's legs vibrated and begged to be found. Closing the door, she went upstairs to freshen up and prepare herself. She took one of her favorite hair ties and twisted her hair up and into a ponytail. Searching for a sexy pair of panties, she closed the drawer, deciding to go without. Then she put on a light blue silk blouse that buttoned and a pair of jeans that fit nicely but had no button and the zipper wouldn't stay up. *Easy access*, she thought. As she walked down the stairs, she took three quick shots of a sweet tasting gin, to lubricate her mind. Her body was already tingling and beginning to drip.

Grabbing her keys and locking up behind herself, she headed next door for the buffet of food and sex.

Chapter 12
The Real Tafts

Alisha sat at the dinner table enjoying the meal of lobster, sweet green beans and the fluffiest mashed potatoes she had ever tasted. The wine she sipped with dinner was kind of dry but was a great booster to the shots from earlier. She and the Tafts conversed in lighthearted conversation as they finished dinner. Finishing the potatoes and most of the lobster, Alisha started to feel a little lightheaded. She figured the wine had fully kicked in until she shifted in her chair and the softness of the seat cushions on her thighs felt like tiny fingers racing to the wishing well between her legs.

"Alisha... dear, are you alright?" Marissa asked with a smile, getting up to move behind her guest.

"Yes, yes, I'm fine... I think. I guess the wine had a stronger effect on me than I thought."

Marissa placed her hands on Alisha's shoulders and began to rub. As she massaged, her hands went down into Alisha's blouse. The feeling of hands against her skin gave off a sensation of unexpected pleasure. When the hands reached her breasts, her nipples shot out, wanting attention too. Alisha laid her head back on the woman's stomach as she enjoyed being felt. Landon got up and stood next to the ladies. He graciously pulled the chair out, with Alisha still in it. He helped her up and she looked deeply into his eyes. He kissed her and his wife joined in and made it a three-way meeting at the lips.

Each of the Tafts took a hand and led Alisha downstairs where the sex room was already prepared and waiting. As they entered, clothes began to hit the floor. Her mind tried to say no, but it couldn't focus on the decision and make her mouth pronounce the words. Her body had taken over and longed to be explored, touched, tasted and used.

They had Alisha reach up to the ceiling and hold on to black velvet, twisted robes. They each took a breast and twirled their tongues on her nipples and sucked like babies with their first taste of mother's milk. Landon lowered himself to her belly and Marissa made her way down her back. Landon parted her feet to better tease the source of the moisture that was now beading up and running down her thigh. Marissa made her way down the back, over, through and past Alisha's toned ass. Then the two mouths met at the lower sweet center.

"Oh, my fucking… more, please, more. Don't stop," Alisha quietly voiced.

Through the licking, Landon said, "Baby, lean her forward and work the outside. I'll go inside."

Alisha pulled herself up off the ground by the ropes when the ecstasy became too great. She lifted her thighs as the atomic orgasm exploded, sending a flood of juicy lust into the Tafts' mouths. They both swallowed what they could and let the rest trickle down their lips. Getting up and helping Alisha keep her balance, they went to the bed.

"I-I feel odd. I mean… what do I mean? What kind of wine was that?"

Neither Taft said anything. They just kissed each other and smiled. Marissa scooted herself up on the bed and sat up with her legs open. Unable to resist, Alisha climbed onto the bed and buried her face between Marissa's inviting thighs. Landon put on a condom and inserted a finger in Alisha's ass. Then two. In and out, faster and faster, until he felt her loosen up. Then he inserted himself inside her anus. Alisha wanted it, but he was too large for that entrance. She tried to take it for as long as she could, but the thrust made her licking become teeth drags.

"Ouch, dear. Landon, you are making her hurt me. She can't take it like I can. Flip her on her back."

"Time to finish already?"

"Yes. Time to finish."

After she was on her back, they tied her wrists to the bed posts. Marissa straddled her face to be licked. Landon lay on top of her, and before sliding in, he quickly removed the condom. Her opening welcomed him inside with warm comfort, juicier and hotter than his wife. As he stroked, he felt himself grow harder than he ever had before. Cupping Alisha's waist, his rhythm increased with speed and force.

"Oh shit, I'm going to come."

Through muffled sound, Alisha announced that she was coming too.

Marissa said, "Wait for me. I'm close now," but through Alisha's body. She felt Landon give his cum thrust and knew he was done. Looking over her shoulder, smiling, she glanced at her husband, but the smile quickly faded to a frown. Rising up, Marissa pulled Landon up off the bed and got in his face.

"I damn well know you didn't just come inside her, you son-of-a-bitch!"

"The condom broke when I started coming."

"You are a fucking liar. The rubber is lying right there." She picked it up and slapped him across the face with it.

"Have you lost your fucking mind?"

"No, but you are about to lose your balls!"

"Wait a minute… hold on. Hold on! Did you forget what is going on here? What damn difference does it make if I bust in this bitch or not?"

"Evidence, dumb ass!"

With her head still in a slight fog, Alisha slowly rolled her head around, trying to focus on something and take control of her body again. The word *evidence* caught her attention. The tingling between her thighs died down as alarm came in. Her wrists were wrapped in some kind of fabric, but it felt like metal. Shaking her arms, she managed to loosen the fabric, to see she was handcuffed to the post on the wall through the bed rails.

"Oh, look who is back to normal. A tad bit too late, though. That Ecstasy we mixed in your potatoes worked quite well. We hope you enjoyed the sex, 'cause that will be the last thing you will enjoy in your last few moments of life," Landon said as he patted her thigh before leaving and continuing his argument with Marissa.

Michael A. Young | 76

Chapter 13

Taft vs. Taft

Muffled words came from outside the door where Alisha was tied. She couldn't exactly tell what they were saying, but she knew they were arguing. Panic tried to snatch her thought process, but this wasn't the time for that. She needed to figure out how she was going to get out of this. It had just become clear that the Tafts' guests might not have been in those bags, but they probably died here, in this room. Giving her environment a quick scan, she noticed dents in the wall behind the bed. Must be where they struggled and caused the posts to slam against the wall. The ceiling had specks of dark spots. Blood spray, more than likely.

"I told you to shut the hell up before you regret it, Marissa! I came in her! So what! Let it go, or else!"

Then Marissa entered the room. "Son-of-a-bitch! We agreed, no bare fucking!"

Then she looked at Alisha. Still lying naked, her body caused Marissa to stare and look her over. "Damn shame to waste such a luscious thing. I don't think I have ever enjoyed a woman as much as I did you," Leaning over, she rubbed her thigh and stopped right before her fingers disappeared inside Alisha.

"I have never been with a woman before. I never knew what I was missing. You made my body dance in ways no song ever did."

"You're just trying to save your life, saying anything."

"Yes, I want to live, but I'm being real. Landon enjoyed me too."

"Bitch, you want to die right away, I see. Mention my husband's name again."

"I'm just telling you what he whispered to me before he left."

"What? What did he say?" The anger changed in her face.

"He mouthed to me that you were the reason I had to go. He would keep me around, cause out of all the women he came in, I made him come the most."

"The most? How many women has he come in?" Marissa asked, not talking to Alisha directly but still looking at her.

"I don't know, but I'm clean. No diseases, and never had one. He is taking a real chance with his and your life. If this was just a sex experience, he jeopardized my life now. How many women have there been? You could be knocking on death's door soon too."

Marissa stood and looked at a spot on the wall then turned slowly towards the door and looked, like she was able to peer through the solid door and see Landon.

"How long will it be before he does catch something? The sex with y'all was amazing. Well, the experience was. You make the connection that takes it to another level. I saw it when y'all were in the backyard—when I was asked to watch with the woman. The encounter I interrupted, checking on YOU! Even after the Ecstasy, it was you who ignited the fire in me."

Looking back at Alisha now, Marissa took in every word she said. Truth was she did enjoy Alisha. Maybe a little too much. Did Landon come in those women? Did he come in those women from where they came here from?

Landon entered the room and looked at the women, first, his wife, then Alisha. Her nude body caused blood to rush back into his weapon. Marissa noticed him get hard after looking at Alisha and not from her.

"What's going on here, going for a round two before it ends?"

"No, fucker. You just want to nut in another woman!"

"Told you to kill that shit. We are not starting that up again."

"You didn't deny it. All those women we had. Did you come in all them? You could have a disease. You could have given it to me!"

Landon had a knife behind his back. He used the arm that held it and pointed at his wife. "Don't keep pissing me off!"

"Or what, Landon?" Then she charged him and they began to tussle by the door. Alisha saw this as her opportunity. Since her legs were free, she kicked them over her head and pushed off the wall, leaving her standing behind it. Since the bed was just a full-size on regular frame and had a rail headboard, it was light enough for her to use her runner's legs and drive the whole bed in the Tafts' direction.

As they argued and wrestled, the Tafts were blindsided by the bed up against the door. Landon slammed his head against the door, stunning him. Marissa fell up against him hard, causing the knife he was holding to go through her chest and heart, killing her instantly. The force she used made Alisha fall through the metal rail headboard, freeing her.

Landon looked down as the body of his lifeless wife fell back onto the bed with the knife deep in her chest. Alisha ran over to him, blasting him in the head with a broken piece of the metal rail that was still attached to her cuffs.

She let go of the weapon and stood over Landon. "You fucked up this time. You had no idea your latest victim was a killer, just like you two. Although you won't be found on the jogging path, you were killed by the same person. Removing the metal spike she'd used to tie up her hair, she stabbed Landon in the side of the head.

Watching the life leave his eyes, she told him, "Looks like you were a victim of the dark side of desire. A mistake you'll never make again." Then she left the basement to call the police. With the multiple dots of blood on the ceiling and probably in the carpet, added to the fact she was still cuffed and had Landon's semen inside her, this was an open and shut case.

Michael A. Young | 84

Chapter 14

Endings

Three days had passed since the police found the Tafts' bodies and the only survivor, Alisha Kriss. The splatters of blood found around the house led police to the names of missing members of the city. Oddly enough, they found that none of them matched any of the bodies found in the park.

Alisha was home because she'd made the news and her job flat out told her to take a vacation— as long as she needed to get herself right. Preparing to go out for a jog and see who was on the trail, the doorbell rang. She opened the door to two detectives and two officers.

"Hello, Ms. Kriss. My name is Detective Melanie Frost, and this is Detective Ra'Neisha Kole, along with officers Young and Wake."

"Okay? Do you need another statement from me?"

Pulling out a couple of clear bags with something in each of them, Detective Kole said, "No, actually, we need to speak to you about your hair tie you used to defend yourself from Mr. Taft."

Looking at the bag, she said, "Yes. That's mine, and what I used to keep him from killing me."

Frost spoke again. "Great! So, the prints on this are yours. And that makes the prints on these spikes we took out of a couple of the victims in the woods murders yours as well. Ms. Kriss, put your hands behind your back. You are under arrest for multiple murders."

The End